GrRrRrRGrRRRRrrr

# HARRY HUNGRY!

Written and illustrated by
**Steven Salerno**

Harcourt, Inc.

Orlando   Austin   New York   San Diego   London

Manufactured in China

"Hungry," Harry murmured. "Harry **HUNGRY**."
His tummy grumbled and rumbled.
"**HUNGRY!**" Harry yelled.

"In a minute," Momma called.

Harry closed his eyes tight.
He raised his fists and opened his mouth wide.
"HUUUNG . . ."

Momma flew into the room with a snack.

Harry gobbled it down!

Momma brought some blueberries.
Harry ate them in a blink!

Momma opened a big box of alphabet
cookies. Harry devoured *A* through *Z*!

He scurried into the kitchen.
Harry pulled open the refrigerator and . . .

ate *everything* inside.

Momma grabbed the phone and called Papa. "Come quickly!" she cried. "It's Harry!"

Harry headed outside.

He ate the flower bed.

He ate the garden hose.

He munched the mailbox!

Papa's car screeched to a halt in the driveway and he hopped out.

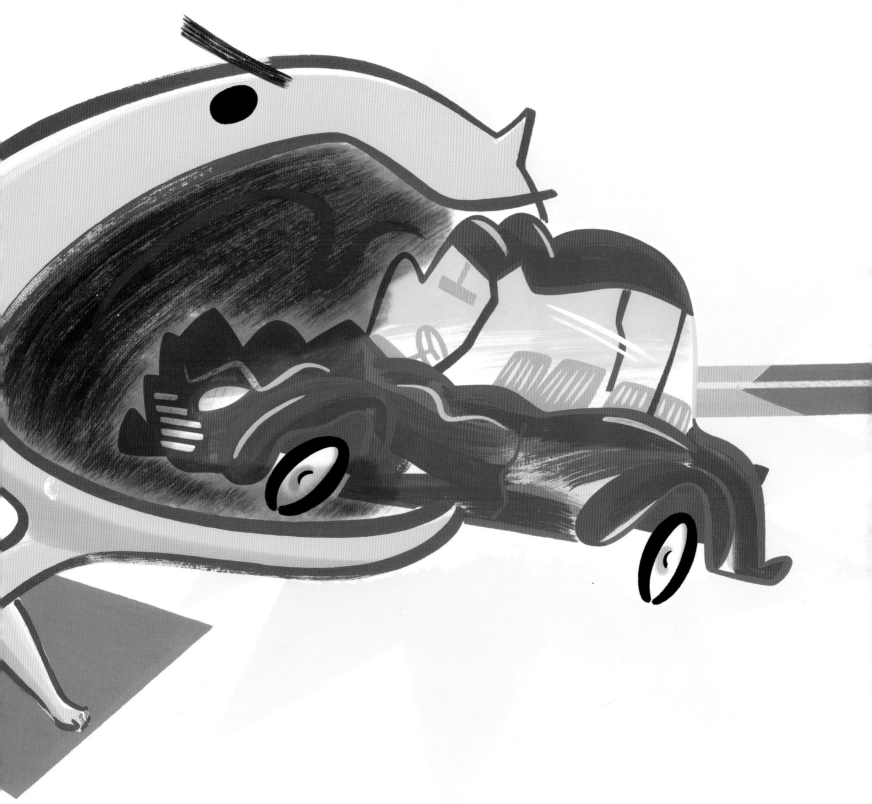

Harry ate the car with a

# CRUNCH!

Momma and Papa pleaded with Harry to stop,
but Harry wouldn't.
Harry *couldn't*!

His tummy grumbled
and rumbled.

GRRRRRRGRRRRRRR

**"HARRY HUNGRY!"** he bellowed.

Harry ate the neighbor's house.

He ate the school.

He took a big bite out of the bridge!

"If we don't do something fast, *nothing* will be left!" shouted Papa.

Harry ate the highway.

He ate the mountain.

He chewed on
a **chunk**
of the
**sky!**

"Call the army, call the navy, we've got
to stop our little Harry!" shouted Momma.

Harry reached
for the moon . . .

and then he wobbled.

GRrRRrRGrrRRRrGrrrR

Harry blinked his eyes, rubbed his nose, and . . .

"Sleepy," said Harry.

Momma and Papa scooped
up Harry and carried him home.

"Shhhhh,"
whispered Papa.

"Sleepy,"
Harry murmured.
"Harry sleepy."

"Hush, Harry," whispered Momma.

And then little Harry fell fast asleep...

until *breakfast*!

For parents who encourage their children
to take a BIG bite out of life

rrrGRRRRRrGrrRRRRRRGrr

Requests for permission to make copies of any part of the work should be submitted
online at www.harcourt.com/contact or mailed to the following address:
Permissions Department, Houghton Mifflin Harcourt Publishing Company,
6277 Sea Harbor Drive, Orlando, Florida 32887-6777.

www.HarcourtBooks.com

Library of Congress Cataloging-in-Publication Data
Salerno, Steven.
Harry hungry!/Steven Salerno.
p.  cm.
Summary: Harry is a baby so hungry that he eats all the food in his house,
then goes outside to find more.
[1. Hunger—Fiction.  2. Food habits—Fiction.  3. Babies—Fiction.]  I. Title.
PZ7.S15212Har  2009
[E]—dc22   2007004375
ISBN 978-0-15-206257-6

First edition
A  C  E  G  H  F  D  B

The illustrations in this book were created using brushes and
Winsor & Newton gouaches on French Aquarelle Arches 260 lb. hot
pressed watercolor paper, with additional enhancements in Photoshop.
The display type was created by Steven Salerno.
The text type was set in Billy.
Color separations by Colourscan Co. Pte. Ltd., Singapore
Manufactured by South China Printing Company, Ltd., China
Production supervision by Christine Witnik
Designed by April Ward and Jennifer Kelly